MOVE OVER, TWERP

Story and pictures by

Martha Alexander

Dial Books for Young Readers

New York

Published by Dial Books for Young Readers
A Division of NAL Penguin Inc.
2 Park Avenue
New York, New York 10016

Published simultaneously in Canada
by Fitzhenry & Whiteside Limited, Toronto
Design by Jane Byers Bierhorst
Printed in the U.S.A.
E
3 5 7 9 10 8 6 4 2

Library of Congress Cataloging in Publication Data
Alexander, Martha G./Move over, Twerp.
SUMMARY: Jeffrey shows his classmates that being
younger and smaller doesn't mean he can be pushed around.
[1. School stories.] I. Title.
PZ7.A3777Mo [E] 80-21405
ISBN 0-8037-6139-2 / ISBN 0-8037-6140-6 (lib. bdg.)

*The art for each picture consists of a
pencil and wash drawing with two color overlays,
all reproduced as halftone.*

For Scott M. S., the real hero of this story

Jeffrey, I'm not going to drive you to school anymore.
I think you're old enough to take the school bus.
Wow! This is the biggest day of my life.

Here it comes, Mom. See you later.

Good morning, sonny. Hop on. You're
my first passenger.

Clear out, Twerp. That's my seat.

I hate the bus. The big kids took my seat.

But weren't there plenty of other seats?
I don't *want* other seats.

But, Dad, they're so big.

Just say, "I will *not* move. I got here first."

Come on, Jeffrey, I'll show you how
to deal with those big kids.
I'll toughen you up.

Just keep thinking to yourself, "I'm the strongest kid in the world. No one can push me around."

Watch me, Jeffrey.

You guys get lost. Take off. You better
not tangle with me.

You can do it, Jeffrey. When you get on that bus, just get in there and fight for your rights.

Thanks, Katie.

But, uh, you know, I got here first, and,
uh, I will not move.

Is that so!

It isn't fair. I've just got to get
my seat back.

I know what I'll do!

Hey, Twerp, you got my seat again. That seat is for big kids.

I'm not moving, and my name isn't Twerp.

It's SUPERTWERP!

YEA! SUPERTWERP! Boy, I wouldn't tangle with *you*.
We better watch this guy. He means business.

So long, Supertwerp.
See you in the morning.

✓